Wordsworth! Stop the Bulldozer!

This book is dedicated to everyone who will join Wordsworth in planting a tree—and to all my nieces and nephews and their children, who gave him their word of honor that they would each plant a tree in his name.

Frances H. Kakugawa

For Emi

Andrew J. Catanzariti

© 2012 Watermark Publishing

Text © 2012 Frances H. Kakugawa

Illustrations © 2012 Andrew J. Catanzariti

ISBN 978-1-935690-30-6

Library of Congress Control Number: 2012947357

Design and production
Jen Tadaki Catanzariti

Watermark Publishing
1088 Bishop Street, Suite 310
Honolulu, HI 96813
Telephone 1-808-587-7766
Toll-free 1-866-900-BOOK
sales@bookshawaii.net
www.bookshawaii.net

Printed in China

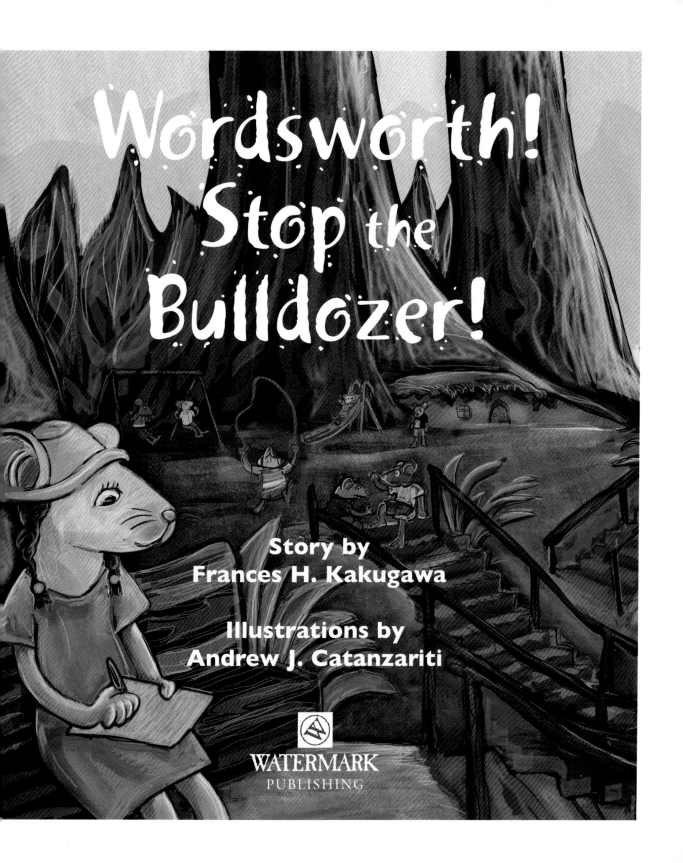

Wordsworth! Stop the Bulldozer!

Story by
Frances H. Kakugawa

Illustrations by
Andrew J. Catanzariti

WATERMARK
PUBLISHING

The Plant A Tree Society

Wordsworth and I created the Plant A Tree Society because we don't want this story to end after the last page. So many trees are being destroyed by bulldozers, and it makes us sad to see them replaced by concrete or asphalt.

Will you join us in making a difference? We have a dream of Wordsworth trees growing in all 50 states and in other countries too, but we need your help. Maybe we can get our communities and our service clubs to join us. How about a Wordsworth tree in every schoolyard? It's not only about trees being cut down where we live. Our children and their children must have trees in their future to hug and enjoy and sit under in the shade. Trees also help keep us alive and healthy. It's something to think about.

For starters, send us a picture of you planting a Wordsworth tree, and we'll mail you a Wordsworth certificate to recognize you as a member of our society. I'll have a special place on my Facebook page where we'll keep a tally of all trees planted.

Your photo with your name and address can be sent by email to Wordsworth@francesk.org or fhk@francesk.org or mailed to Watermark Publishing, 1088 Bishop Street, Suite 310, Honolulu, HI 96813.

—*Frances H. Kakugawa*

Dear Readers,

Here it is, the third Wordsworth book I promised you. I hope you enjoy this story and the poems.

You will recognize some haiku poems; they are written in three lines with 17 syllables in this order: 5, 7, 5.

You will also meet my new friend Akiko. She writes tanka poems. Tanka poems were first written in ancient Japan before haiku was introduced. Tanka poems have 5 lines with 31 syllables in this order: 5-7-5-7-7

Now for some good news: My first book, *Wordsworth the Poet*, won the Hawai'i Book Publishers Association's Award of Excellence in 2004. My second book, *Wordsworth Dances the Waltz*, won the Northern California Publishers/ Authors' award for Best Children's Book of 2008. That was very exciting.

I keep all of your emails and letters in my special shoebox. Please write to me at the addresses below because I read your letters over and over again. I promise to answer all of my mail. You can also check me out on Frances H. Kakugawa's website and on Facebook.

Thank you, dear readers!

Frances' website: www.francesk.org
Frances' Facebook Page: www.facebook.com/FrancesKakugawa
Wordsworth's Facebook Page: www.facebook.com/WordsworthThePoet
Wordsworth's email: Wordsworth@francesk.org
Or care of Watermark Publishing, 1088 Bishop Street, Suite 310, Honolulu, HI 96813

Poor Wordsworth. His best friend, Emily, was gone. Emily's family had moved from their home in Hawai'i to far-off Maine two weeks ago, during spring vacation. Today was the first day back in school after he and Emily had said goodbye. Walking to school, Wordsworth didn't see the flowers in bloom or feel the soft breeze on his face. He felt he was a large jigsaw puzzle with one piece missing. He slipped his hand into his pocket and carefully put his fist around a folded sheet of paper on which he had scribbled a poem about Emily.

Missing Emily

My 100-piece jigsaw puzzle
Is missing one piece.
All 99 pieces
Fit snugly in place.
Edges cornered, lined,
Ready for completion.
But in the center is a space
For that one final piece.
But that piece is gone,
Leaving the puzzle
Incomplete.
Unfinished.
Broken.

Wordsworth gasped when he entered his classroom. Someone was sitting in Emily's chair! Before he could give her a good look, or even think of how he felt seeing someone sitting there, the bell rang. "Good morning, boys and girls," the teacher began. "I have a wonderful surprise this morning. We have a new student. This is Akiko. Akiko is a student from Japan. Please introduce yourself and welcome Akiko to our class during recess."

When the bell rang for recess, Eliot and Dylan walked outside with Wordsworth. Dylan, who had crowned himself the class clown, looked at Wordsworth's face and was quiet. Eliot noticed the new student sitting by herself. "Let's go talk to her," he told his two friends.

"Yes," added Wordsworth. "I wonder what it's like to be a new student. Emily's a new student today in Maine. Maybe if we talk to Akiko, someone will be speaking to Emily, too." Eliot, with his crinkly whiskers, knew all about being a new student and hurried toward Akiko with Dylan and Wordsworth.

"Hi Akiko," began Eliot. "I'm Eliot and this is Wordsworth and Dylan. Tell us about Japan. What do you do during recess? Do you just hang around like us or do you play Japanese games? How about teaching us something Japanese?"

Akiko stood up and said, "I'm very happy to meet you. My father said I must forget being Japanese while I'm here and to be more American. Maybe you can teach me to become more American."

"I don't know how to do that," said Eliot.

"Well," Dylan said with a chuckle, "for starters, how about shaking hands?" All three boys shook hands with Akiko, laughing along with her.

Wordsworth looked at Akiko, "Maybe you should be Japanese for a few more weeks. We're writing haiku poems in class next week. I heard students learn to write poems when they're very young in Japan. Is that right? Do you write poems?"

"Yes, I learned to write them in first grade and I still do."

"Uh-oh," said Dylan. "Now we have two poets. Wordsworth is a poet, too, Akiko. Ask him to show you some of his poems. He helps us see things that we miss. In fact, he's got that look on his face right now. I think he's writing a poem in his head."

Dylan was right. Wordsworth was thinking about Akiko trying not to be Japanese. Emily was no longer in Hawai'i. "I hope Emily is still being Emily even if she's not here." In a way, it reminded him of all the fun he had dancing with his grandma, who was becoming very forgetful these days. Yet in spite of this, Wordsworth knew he would always be part of his grandma's life.

Roots

Roots from the oak
Grow down deep.
We are acorns
From the great oak.

The end-of-recess bell jolted him back to the conversation. Dylan and Eliot were asking Akiko for her home address so they could all spend time together on the weekend.

That Saturday, after their karate lessons, Wordsworth, Dylan and Eliot stopped by Akiko's house to invite her to explore the neighborhood with them. They passed Emily's old house and no one said anything. They came to a lumberyard. Akiko closed her eyes and said, "I love the smell of freshly cut wood. My grandfather built a beautiful minka for us to live in. I would get up early to listen to the sound of grandfather sawing and shaping lumber for our minka. After a while, I could tell the difference between cherry, pine and other woods just by their smell."

"What's a minka?" asked Eliot.

Before Akiko could explain the Japanese wooden farmhouse that was built without nails, Dylan shouted, "Let's go inside!" They followed him through the gate and wandered among the stacks of lumber. Running his hand across a large plank, Wordsworth wondered aloud, "Just think, this piece of wood was once part of a huge tree."

"Look at the lines on that lumber," Eliot said. "Is that beautiful or what? How did these lines happen?"

"It's called the grain of the wood," Wordsworth explained. "Different woods have different grains. If you cut a tree across the trunk, this line here is part of the ring that shows the tree's annual growth. Each year, one ring, like a clock that only ticks once every 365 days."

Dylan touched a piece of knotty pine. "How about this? How did this knot get in here?"

"That's where a branch grew out of the tree and became part of it, Wordsworth explained. "See that knot in the middle? When the tree was younger, that branch started to grow and it was on the outside of the tree. As the tree grew, the branch kept growing, too. The tree grew around the branch. The knot you see is the branch."

"What? I thought someone pounded it in," Dylan said with a smile. "Wordsworth, how do you know all this stuff?"

"Oh, I read it in a book," he said.

Eliot was already walking away. "Hey, let's see how many different kinds of trees we can see in all this lumber." They walked around the stacks and began calling out the names of the different trees: redwood, birch, pine, oak, cedar, maple, Hawaiian koa. Before long they were running through the aisles exclaiming, "I see a cypress tree in this wood!"—naming trees they pretended to see, until a foreman shouted, "Hey, you kids don't belong here!"

"Just imagine," said Wordsworth, as they hurried out. "Imagine a house built with live trees." Akiko murmured, "I know someone who already lives in a house of living trees."

The four friends, buried in their own thoughts and images, walked home in silence. Someone muttered, "A house made without dead trees." It was Wordsworth who later captured their afternoon in a haiku poem he called "Tree House."

Tree House

Eucalyptus trees
Clear visions of koalas
Playing on our porch.

Our new wooden floors
Of stately green pine bringing
Christmas all year round.

Wall after wall of
Redwood trees surround, protect,
To keep us warm, safe.

Two fans whir and spin
From mighty oak-beam ceilings.
Where are the acorns?

Cedar shakes, shingles'
Sweet drops of fragrant forest
Rain, drip from our roofs.

Welcome to my house
Made without blueprints or saws.
Would you like some juice?

Wordsworth lay in bed that night thinking of all the changes in his life. His mind felt like a kaleidoscope of thoughts and ideas. "Emily is gone but I still think of her every day. I hear her voice whispering in the wind, 'Wordsworth, you are a poet.' Emily will always be my special friend."

Thoughts of Emily led to thoughts of the quiet Hawaiian koa grove where they had spent so many hours under a certain tree. Emily loved to hug that koa tree. Will it still be there tomorrow? The lumber at the lumberyard was once beautiful, majestic trees, homes for birds and other animals. Today, all that beautiful wood lay in the lumberyard like fallen soldiers. Maybe some-day, new trees would grow toward the blue sky in the same places where the others had been. Wordsworth couldn't imagine a world without trees, no more than he could imagine a world without friends.

In early December, Akiko invited Wordsworth to her house to show him her collection of poems. At first he wanted to say yes, but he thought of the letter in his pocket. Wordsworth explained he had somewhere to go and walked off toward the koa grove, which was now his favorite place to be alone. In his pocket, he had a letter from Emily which was refolded many times over. He knew the letter by heart:

Dear Wordsworth,

I made my first snowman today with two of our neighbors. I call him Snowy the Poet. Snowy even has one of your poems in his hand. I wish you could see what snow does to a place. Winter in Maine is a place for poets, Wordsworth, especially in the morning when the snow is fresh and there isn't a mark on the snowy ground. Wordsworth, I can hear the silence.

Say hello to Eliot and Dylan. I miss going to karate classes with all of you. And I miss you and your poems.

Love,
Emily

P.S. I sent you a book about trees.

Wordsworth walked to the grove with one hand in his pocket. He stopped and stared. "No, this can't be! Am I dreaming? I must be in the wrong place!" He looked around, confused. "Where are all the koa trees?" He blinked his eyes twice. Except for one tree, the rest of the grove was gone. Then he saw what had happened.

A bulldozer was parked among the fallen trees piled high on one side of the grove. On the other side was a flatbed truck loaded with logs.

Wordsworth climbed up the flatbed to sit on top of the dead trees. He sat for what seemed like hours with his pen in his hand, but the words for Emily wouldn't come. For the first time, he was at a loss for words. He sat and looked at what used to be his favorite place. After a while, he put his pen and blank sheet of paper back into his pocket.

Suddenly, without warning, he heard the bulldozer at the edge of what was once a beautiful koa grove, coming to life like a sleeping beast roaring, roaring, "Grrrung... Grrrung..."

The bulldozer began to grate and grind, a menacing, smoking dragon, slowly shoving the uprooted trees out of its way. It moved like a river of lava, inch by inch, toward the last standing tree. "Oh no!" Wordsworth thought. "Not that tree! Emily and I carved our initials in it! That's our tree!"

He jumped down from the flatbed and ran toward the tree. Grrrung. Grrrung. The bulldozer moved closer. Wordsworth ran faster. Grrrung. Grrrung. The bulldozer inched ever closer. Wordsworth ran like a sprinter at the Olympics. Finally, he stood between the bulldozer and the tree, gasping for breath. He waved his hands frantically, shouting,

"Stop the bulldozer! Stop the bulldozer!"
The driver looked at Wordsworth. "What's wrong?" he
called, straining to hear what Wordsworth was yelling at him.

"Stop your grating and your grinding.
Take this dragon out of here.
You knocked down trees,
Flowers and vines.
You destroyed
My special place.
Save this tree,
Oh, save this tree.
Stop, you dragon!
Before it's too late."

The bulldozer sputered and groaned. The bucket came down with a thud one last time as if in great pain.

The 'dozer crawled to a complete stop. The driver looked at Wordsworth. Wordsworth looked at the driver. The driver shook his head, climbed out of the cab of the bulldozer and walked off to find his foreman.

Wordsworth just stood there in amazement. He heard the driver say to his foreman, "Get yourself another driver. I'm not about to knock down that kid's tree."

Wordsworth was stunned. "What did I do?" he asked himself. "What did I do?"
    Suddenly he heard applause and shouting behind him. "Way to go, Wordsworth, way to go!" It was Eliot, Dylan and Akiko, standing and clapping and cheering for Wordsworth. Sheepishly, he joined the friends who had seen what he had done and they all walked home, talking and laughing excitedly:

Stop the Bulldozer.
Stop the Dragon.
Save this tree,
Before it's too late.
Sputter, sputter, sput-sput-sput!"

Alone in his room that night, Wordsworth thought of the koa grove that was no longer there. It had been such a special place. He felt sad and angry all at the same time. "My private place where I went to write my poems is gone. I wonder what will be built on that flattened grove?" Little comfort came to Wordsworth even after writing a poem.

The Bulldozer

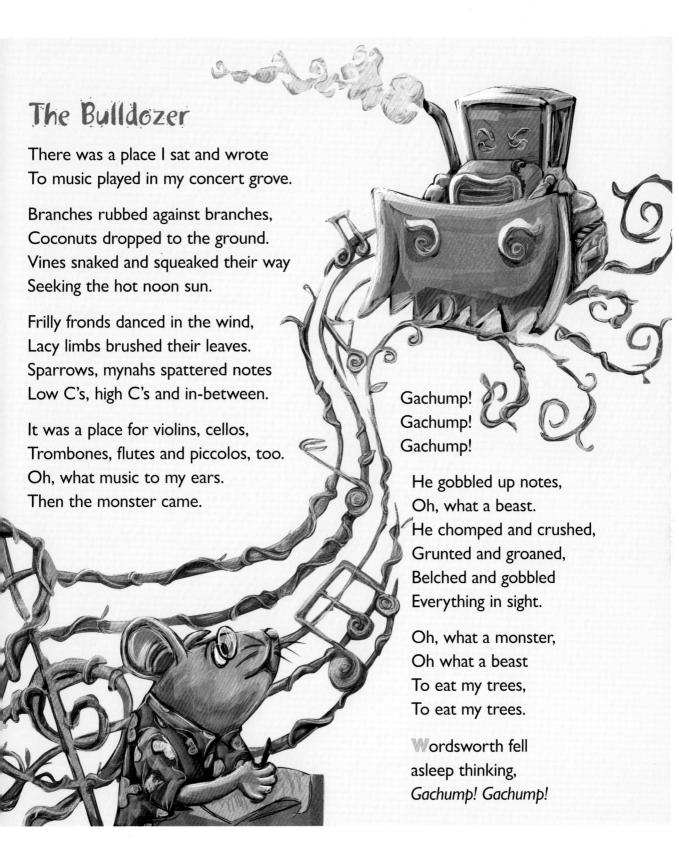

There was a place I sat and wrote
To music played in my concert grove.

Branches rubbed against branches,
Coconuts dropped to the ground.
Vines snaked and squeaked their way
Seeking the hot noon sun.

Frilly fronds danced in the wind,
Lacy limbs brushed their leaves.
Sparrows, mynahs spattered notes
Low C's, high C's and in-between.

It was a place for violins, cellos,
Trombones, flutes and piccolos, too.
Oh, what music to my ears.
Then the monster came.

Gachump!
Gachump!
Gachump!

He gobbled up notes,
Oh, what a beast.
He chomped and crushed,
Grunted and groaned,
Belched and gobbled
Everything in sight.

Oh, what a monster,
Oh what a beast
To eat my trees,
To eat my trees.

Wordsworth fell
asleep thinking,
Gachump! Gachump!

One day a few days later, Wordsworth was thinking about Akiko. "Akiko is not Emily," he thought, "but she's becoming a good friend." He decided to visit her. He walked over to her house and knocked on the front door. "How are you doing, Akiko?" he asked when she let him in.

"I'm fine most of the time," she answered. "Sometimes I feel homesick for my grandmother who's still in Japan. Sometimes I miss our old house." They sat on the couch in her living room. "I wrote these two tanka poems this morning. This is about our fish pond."

Fish Pond

How still the waters.
A red koi moves lazily.
Pink cherry blossoms
Slowly float to block my view.
Oh Mr. Koi, where are you?

I dip my bare toes
Sending ripples in the pond.
Ah, how cool my toes.
A splash of red suddenly
Nips my toe and disappears.

"And this is about my
grandmother," she said.

A Memory

Hot boiling green tea
Poured from a porcelain pot
Sends white fragrant steam
Up to my grandmother's face,
Clouding her round eyeglasses.

"Grandmother," I laugh,
"I cannot see your two eyes,
The tea is too hot."
"Ah, Akiko, Akiko,
I see you even through clouds."

Akiko noticed Wordsworth was not saying a word. She looked at him and put her poems away. "Wordsworth, why do you look so sad? Is it my poems?"

"No," Wordsworth said, but he still looked sad.

"Come on, Wordsworth," Akiko suggested, "Let's go for a walk." She led the way toward the grove that was no more. When they neared the place, they heard voices. It was Dylan and Eliot, laughing and telling stories near the lone koa tree.

"Hey Wordsworth," Dylan shouted," We went to your house but you were out. Hey, why so glum?"

"Yeah," Eliot added, "You look like you lost your best friend."

"Oh, I don't know," Wordsworth tried to explain. "Maybe it's that tree."

"But Wordsworth!" Akiko said, "That was brave what you did. You saved this tree. You stopped the bulldozer."

"I didn't do anything, Akiko. Tomorrow or the next day or even next year, this might be a parking lot. I can't stop all the bulldozers."

"I don't think you're expected to stop all the bulldozers, Wordsworth," Akiko said.

"Hey!" Eliot exclaimed, standing up. "Maybe we can do something to stop the bulldozers."

"I know!" said Dylan excitedly. "Let's go see the mayor and tell him to stop the bulldozers."

"No, let's go to the governor and tell him to declare Save A Tree Day," laughed Akiko.

Wordsworth joined in, shouting, "Let's go to the White House and see the President! Stop the bulldozers, Mr. President!"

They all began laughing again as friends do, except for Akiko, who had become quiet. "Do you all have the haiku poems you wrote in school?" she asked. "Will you let me have a copy of your poems?"

"Why?" Dylan asked. "Are you going to stop the bulldozers with our poems?" They laughed and poked one another.

"Sure, you can have them," said Wordsworth. "We'll go get them right now." And so they did, but not before making a date to meet the following Saturday for a swim.

Come Saturday morning, the four friends headed toward the beach. Something strange was going on as they walked down the road. Wordsworth was the first to notice. He stopped and pointed at a tree in a neighbor's yard. "Look," Wordsworth pointed, "What's that?"

Eliot said, "There's a sheet of paper taped on the tree. Look, there's a paper on every tree! What's going on?" People were coming out of their houses to read what was on those papers, all abuzz about something. What was happening?

They ran toward the nearest tree. Eliot whispered, "Wordsworth, it's your haiku."

One of the neighbors said, "You know, I never paid much attention to this tree. But see what it says here." She looked down at the nuts lying on the ground. "I didn't know these were kukui nuts."

"Yes," another neighbor replied. "The old Hawaiians called this candlenut tree a kukui tree. They used the nuts and trees for oil, medicine and canoes. The bulldozers are going to cut this tree down to widen the road. But we have to help save it. It's part of our history."

Save This Tree

Great great-grandfather
Picked kukui nuts right here
To lighten dark nights.

The voices sounded like honey bees buzzing in a hive. Wordsworth heard words like "the City Council, "neighborhood board" and "the mayor's office."

Wordsworth walked up to another tree, coconut this time. "Eliot, this is your poem."

Save This Tree

High among the fronds,
I taste coconut cream pie.
Watch out below! Thump!

As they walked from tree to tree, they listened to people talking about the poems and the trees. One of Dylan's haiku was taped on a pine tree. Akiko's tanka poem was on a mango tree. The titles were all the same: "Save This Tree."

Save This Tree

Wow! I feel Christmas
Three hundred sixty-five days,
Smelling fresh green pine.

Save This Tree

Pickled green mangoes,
Homemade chutney with raisins.
Best of all, my face
In a ripe mango, juices
Dripping down my chin.

33

"Who did this?" one of the neighbors asked, looking around at all the trees now surrounded by adults conversing in low voices. Akiko and the boys didn't say anything, although they all knew the answer. Wordsworth, Dylan and Eliot turned to look at Akiko, who was smiling and blushing. Wordsworth whispered, "Thank you, Akiko."

Akiko nodded and said, "But I ran out of poems. There are many more trees on this road."

"I know, let's ask everyone in our class to join us. We can do that on Monday."

"We can write stories, too, about our favorite tree."

"Wow! I didn't think we could really make a difference!"

"I think we just did!"

"Hey, race you to the beach!"

"Last one in is a rotten bulldozer!"

Wordsworth watched as the others raced ahead of him. He didn't mind that they'd call him a bulldozer when he was the last to arrive. He stood there looking at the people still gathered by the trees.

"What would happen," he said to himself, "if all the poets in the world wrote poems to save our forests, rivers, animals, earth, air and oceans? Wouldn't that be something?"

And with that, he ran to join the others, and soon the four good friends, all talking at once, were racing into the ocean.

A chorus of their voices rose above the sound of the waves rolling toward shore.

Stop the bulldozers!

Stop the dragon!
Save a tree
Before it's too late.
Sputter, sputter, sput-sput-sput!